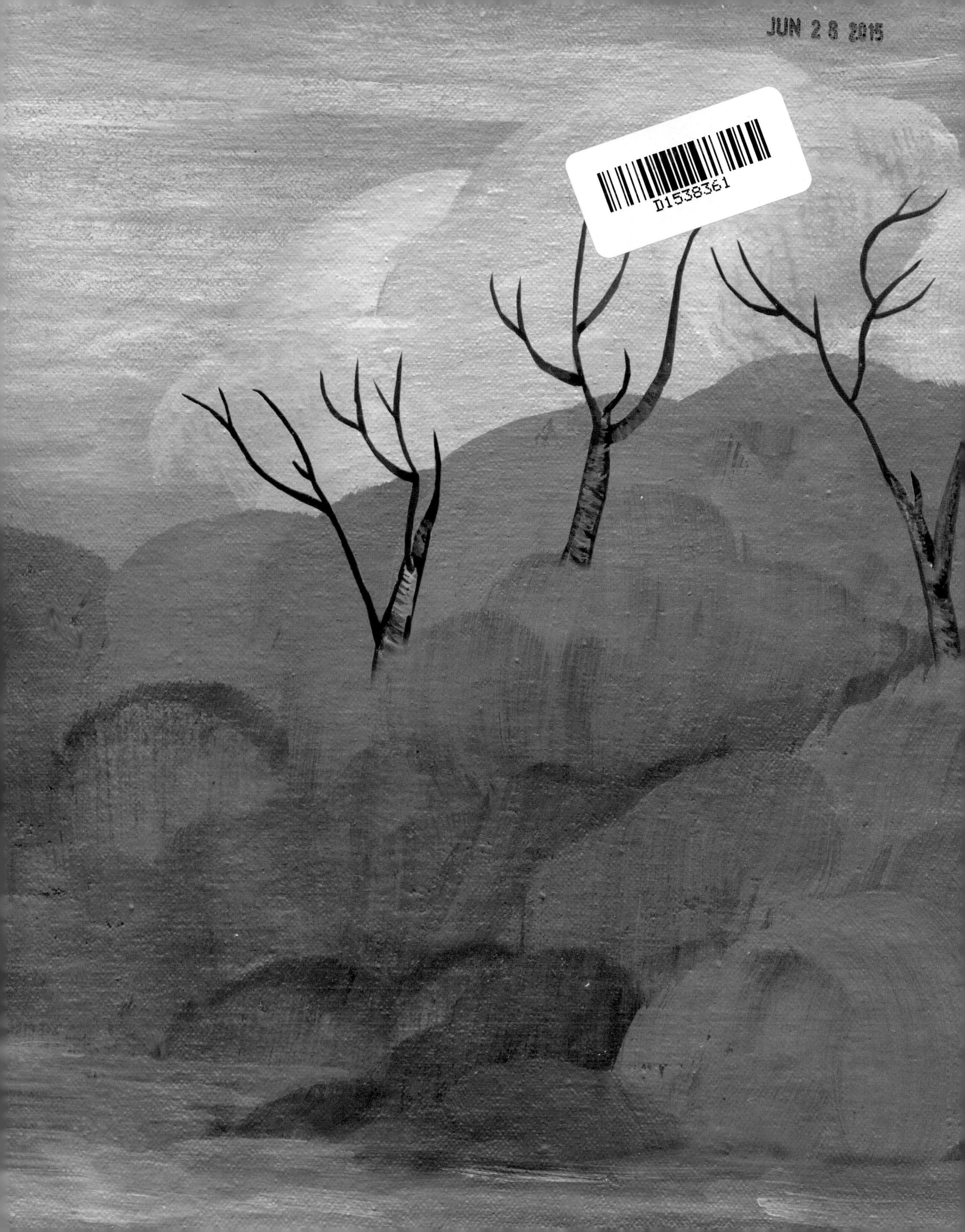

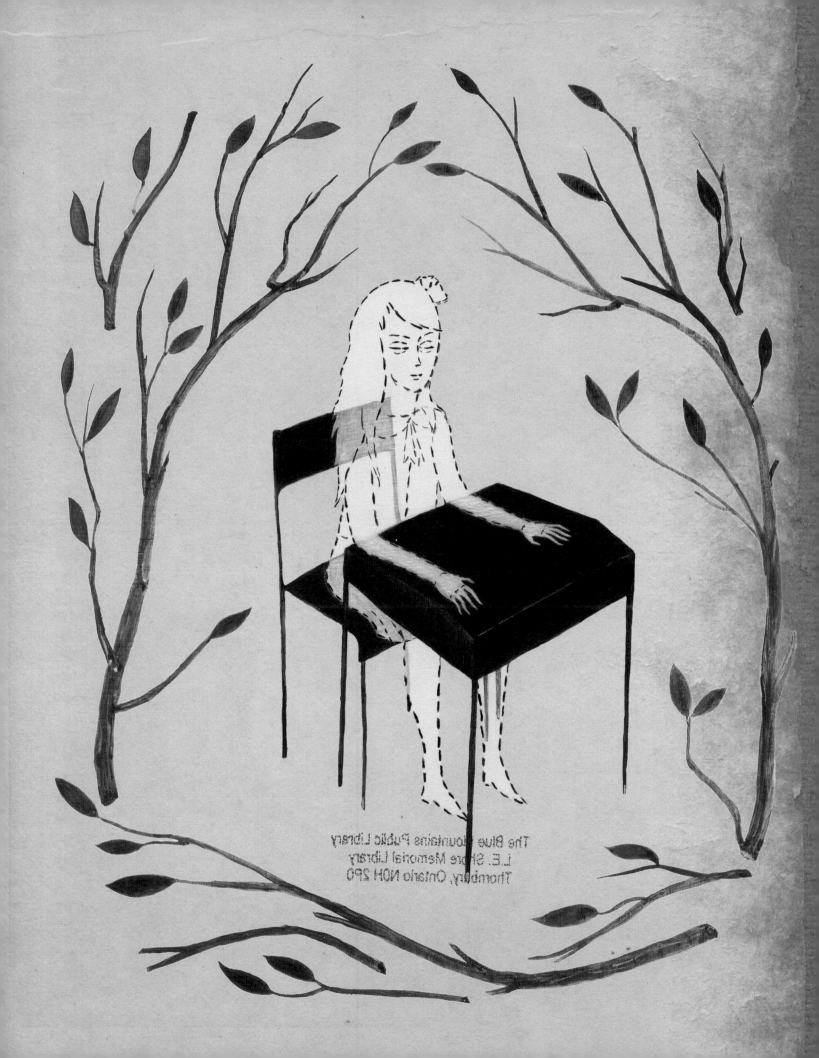

REBECCA CHAPERON

EERIE DEARIES

26 WAYS TO
MISS SCHOOL

SIMPLY READ BOOKS

Dedicated to Gwendolen & Benjamin,
my greatest allies in all that I do.

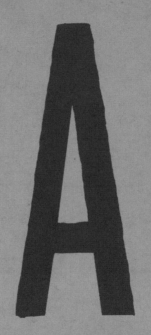

is for
ASTRAL PROJECTION

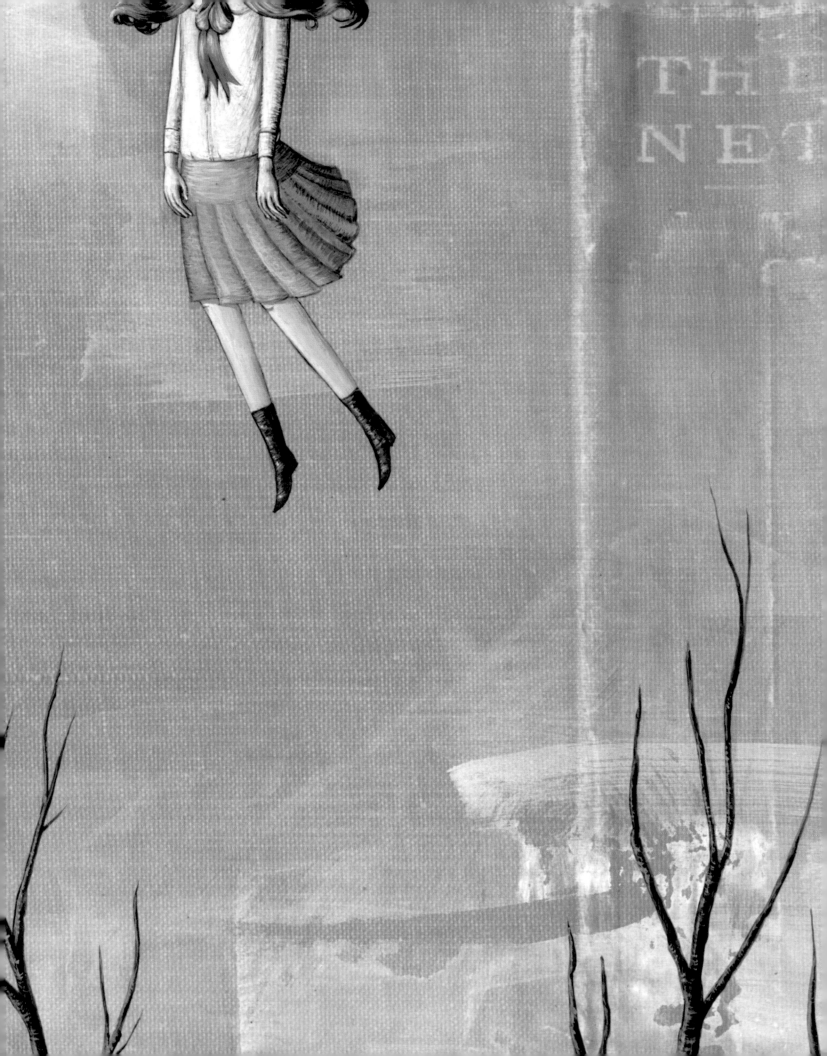

B

is for

BROKEN HEART

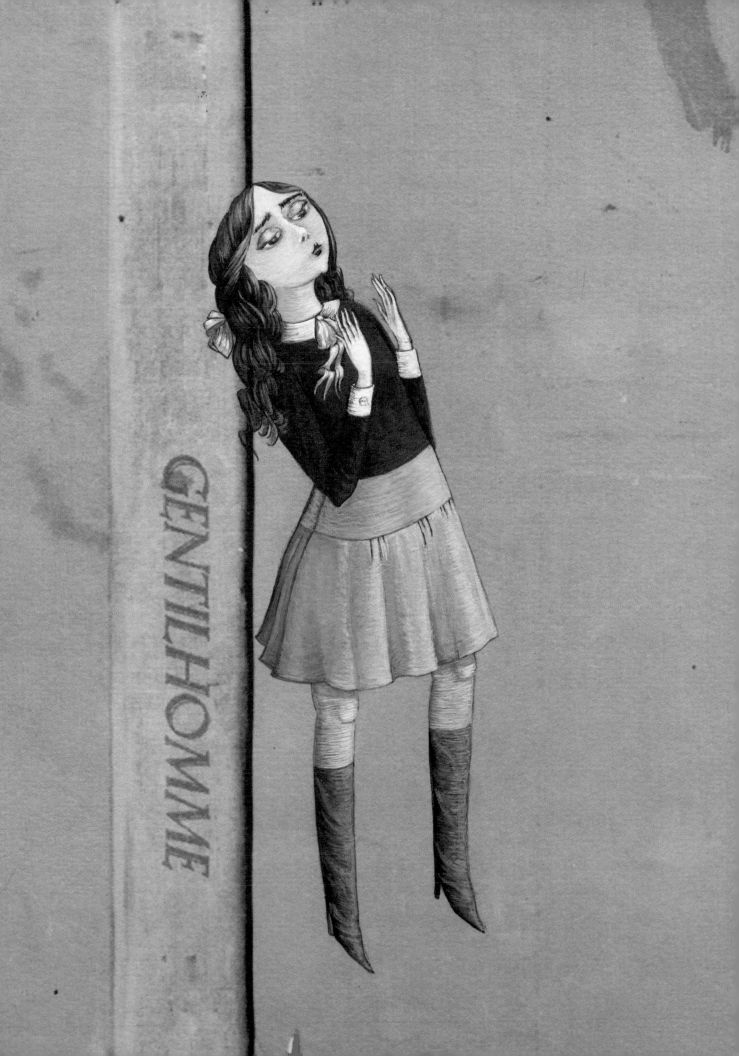

C

is for

CONTAGIOUS

Twenty Letters to a Friend

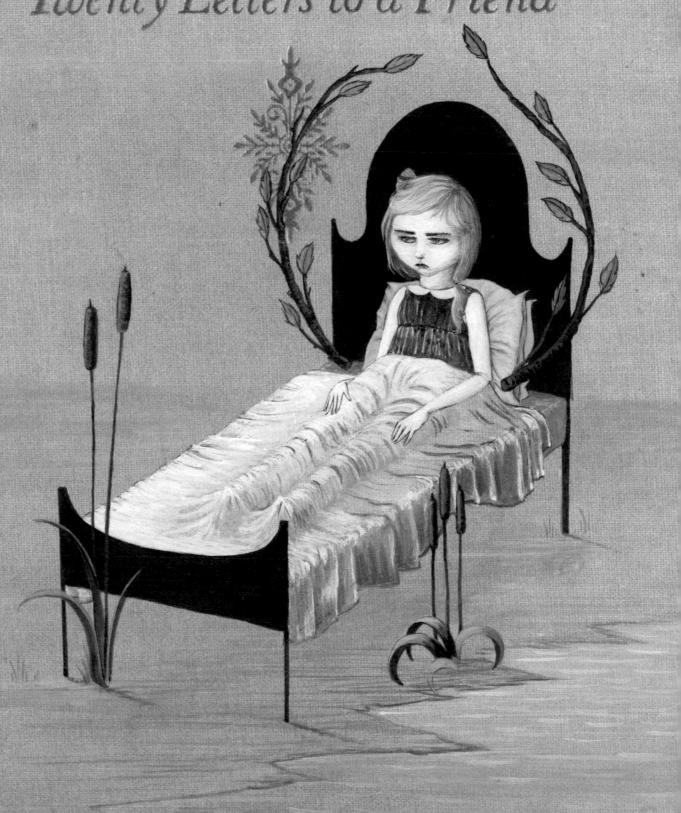

D

is for

DUMBSTRUCK

INDEX

PAGE

Advice, Siddy's 374
Aid for the Sick 670
All like a Dream 368
Amateur Art Exhibition, Our 480
AMATEUR PHOTOGRAPHY :—
  Instantaneous Photography .. 347
  Portraiture 595
American Namesake, Exeter's 602
April, Our Garden in .. 288
Arcadie, A Maid of .. 122
Armstrong, Sir W. G., and Newcastle .. .. ..
Art, A Morning at the Female School of .. 215
Art Exhibition, Our Amateur 480
Art of Garnishing, The .. 878
Art of Making Pictures in Stone, The.. .. 6
Art of Soup-Making, The .. 35
Artists, Pavement .. ..
At a College Breakfast Party 247
Atlantic Telegraphy, The Story of 59
August, The Garden in .. 528
"Auld Robin Gray," The Story of .. ..
Australian Forest, In an ..

Baby and I, My .. 5
Battle that all must Fight, A 60
Behind the Tapestry .. 2
Belgian Holiday, A .. 80, 159
Bengal, Home Life in .. 491
Berlin Castle, The White Lady of the 568
Best Estate, The 670
Birthday Cards, How to Paint Christmas and .. 18
Birthday Party, Eric's .. 478
Blind Man's Song, A .. 570
Bread, Old, and New .. 725
Breakfast Party, At a College 247
Bridesmaids, Old Notions concerning 688
BY-PATHS OF COMMERCE :— Rags and the Trade in them 154

Canning House, A Visit to a (Sights and Scenes of the New World) 558
Canoe Voyage down the Wharfe, A 651
Cards, How to Paint Christmas and Birthday.. .. 18
Catching the Post .. 157
Certificated Teacher," "Wanted, a 693
Chairman, Mr. 747
Cheerful Patient, My .. 606
Children's Room, The .. 107
China, Concerning Derby .. 500
Chinese Newspaper, A .. 94
CHIT-CHAT ON DRESS, (WHAT TO WEAR) 43, 119, 183, 243, 311, 371, 427, 495, 555, 632, 695, 756
Christian Name, How to Choose a 542
Christmas and Birthday Cards, How to Paint .. 18
CLASP, WITHIN THE 1, 65, 129, 193, 257, 321, 385, 449, 513, 577, 641, 705, 756
Clay, Modelling in, as a Remunerative Employment.. 152
Club, How to Form a Tricycle.. 401
Coal, The Real Cost of .. 398

PAGE

COMPETITIONS, PRIZE :— 64, 128, 14?, 192, 256, 320, 353, 384, 448, 576, 640, 704
Concerning Derby China .. 500
Continental Trips as a Means of Education .. 464
COOKERY, PAPERS ON :—
  How to Cook Potatoes .. 30

Dream, All Like a ..
DRESS, WHAT TO WEAR, CHIT-CHAT ON 43, 119, 183, 243, 311, 371, 427, 495, 555, 632, 695, 756
Earthquake Experiences, Our 498
Eating and Drinking, An Invalid's 537
Education, Continental Trips as a Means of .. 464
Elders, How We Entertained our 440
EMPLOYMENTS FOR GENTLEMEN, REMUNERATIVE, 117, 225, 366, 502
EMPLOYMENTS FOR GENTLEWOMEN, REMUNERATIVE 53, 174, 305, 438, 562, 682
Endings of Letters, On the 97
Endings of Things, On the 736
Engineering College, Cooper's Hill 716
England, How, Strikes a Colonist .. 339, 591
England, More Impressions ..

PAGE

Fables, Some Modern 35, 155
"Faint Heart Ne'er Won Fair Lady" (Prize Story) 74?
Fair Margaret .. 442
FAMILY DOCTOR, PAPERS BY A (see under "Docto")
FAMILY PARLIAMENT, THE
  Are We Over-Educating Children? .. 249
  Ought the State to Provide Healthy Homes for the Poor 300, 494
..uary, Our Garden in 39
..le School of Art, A
..orning at the .. 215
..ey (A Nineteenth Century Holiday Resort 639
Fil.. La .. 528
.. to Fin 469
.. 413
.. 738
..australia 271
..orget 186
..ax to Fi
.. 469
Our, in Janua 92
  " Febru 139
  " Marc 20?
  " April 28
.. 34
.. 40
..ntning 320
..Boxes 636
Asbestos Enamel .. 190
Asphalte Mortar .. 192
Balance, Magnetic .. 318
Balance, Parcels Post .. 251
Balloon, New .. 381
Balloon, Propelling .. 764
Barnet's Accumulator .. 316
Barometer, Natural .. 318
Batteries, Lighting Cars by 192
Battery, Gold .. 571
Battery, Pocket .. 316
Battery, Sunlight .. 251
Beacons, Self-Lighting .. 637
Bed Railway Carriages .. 639
Bell, New .. 575
Bell, Portable Electric .. 576
Bell, Water .. 764
Bicycle Bell, Electric .. 381
Biological Station, British 701
Blast Furnace Slag, New Use for 59
Bleaching Sponges .. 125
Boiler, Coking .. 126
Boilers, Cast-Iron .. 508
Boilers, Catechu and .. 189
Boilers, Lighting .. 190
Book-Clip .. 762
Book-Rest, Useful .. 443
Boot-Label .. 760

PAGE

THE GATHERER—Continued.

Cable Tramway, New .. 571
Candlestick, Pocket .. 316
Carbonic Acid, Solid .. 509
Cartoons, Compound .. 576
Carcases, Utilising .. 63
Carpet Fastener .. 255
Carriages, Steel-framed .. 253
Cars, Lighting, by Batteries 192
Cast-Iron Boilers .. 508
Catechu and Boilers .. 189
Cedar-Paper.. .. 383
Centre-Cycle .. 380
Chain Coal Loop .. 317
Chain, Monster .. 62
Chair, Crystal .. 319
Chicken-Hatcher, Electric 635
China Vase, The Largest, in the World 572
Churn, Marble .. 704
Circle, Squaring the .. 760
City Fire Alarms .. 59
Clip, Book .. 762
Cleansing of Waste-Pipes 126
Clock, Sun-Wound .. 188
Clock, Water .. 384
Coal, Manitoban .. 251
Coat and Hat Rack, Pocket 384
Coal-Loop, Chain .. 317
Coke, Natural .. 508
Coking Boiler .. 126
Cold, Effect of on Microbes 508
Colour Combiner .. 635
Coloured Photographs on Glass 189
Colours Photographed in Natural Shades 638
Compass 188
Conductor, Electric Light .. 509
Conduits for Electric Wires, Granolithic 127
Cork Floater, Handy .. 383
Coronator 253
Cremation, Sewer-Gas .. 701
Crystal Chair .. 319
Cure.. Steamed or Frosty Gl.. .. 576

Damp-proof Paint 704
Damp from Flies .. 511
Deep Sea Fishes, New .. 440
Des.. ppetiser, Watch .. 509
Disinfecting Oven .. 62
Distance Judger .. 763
Distributing Electricity .. 575
Door-Handle, New .. 316
Doors, Motion .. 703
.. .. 127
.. .. 383
.. Useful .. 125
.. Cut Flowers .. 252
.. and the Telegraph .. 510
Earthquake Recorder .. 639
Effects of Cold on Microbes 508
Effects of Pressure on Life 444
Eggs, Preserved .. 637
Electric Bell, Portable .. 576
Electric Bicycle Bell .. 381
Electric Chicken-Hatcher 635
Electric Firelock .. 254
Electric Gas-Tap and Lighter 442
Electric Governor .. 762
Electric Insect .. 386
Electric Jewels .. 254
Electric Lamp, Submarine 574
Electric Light Conductors 509
Electric Light Effects 572
Electric Light from the Seine 380
Electric Light Holders 61
Electric Light, New Applications of .. 512
Electric Light Spectacles 700
Electric Light, Travelling 190
Electric Light Wires, Lightning and 702
Electric Line, One-Rail .. 573
Electric Microscope .. 381
Electric Mountain Railway 511
Electric Parcels Post .. 760
Electric Table Fan .. 117
Electric Water-Alarm .. 636
Electric Wire-Rope Railway 95
Electric Wire Transport 256
Electric Wires, Granolithic Conduits for 127
Electrical Actinometer .. 701
Electrical Speed Indicator 124
Electrical Watch .. 87
Electricity and Friction .. 191
Electricity and Tanning .. 11?

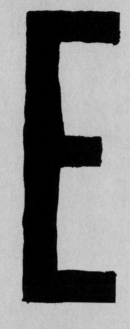

is for

ENNUI

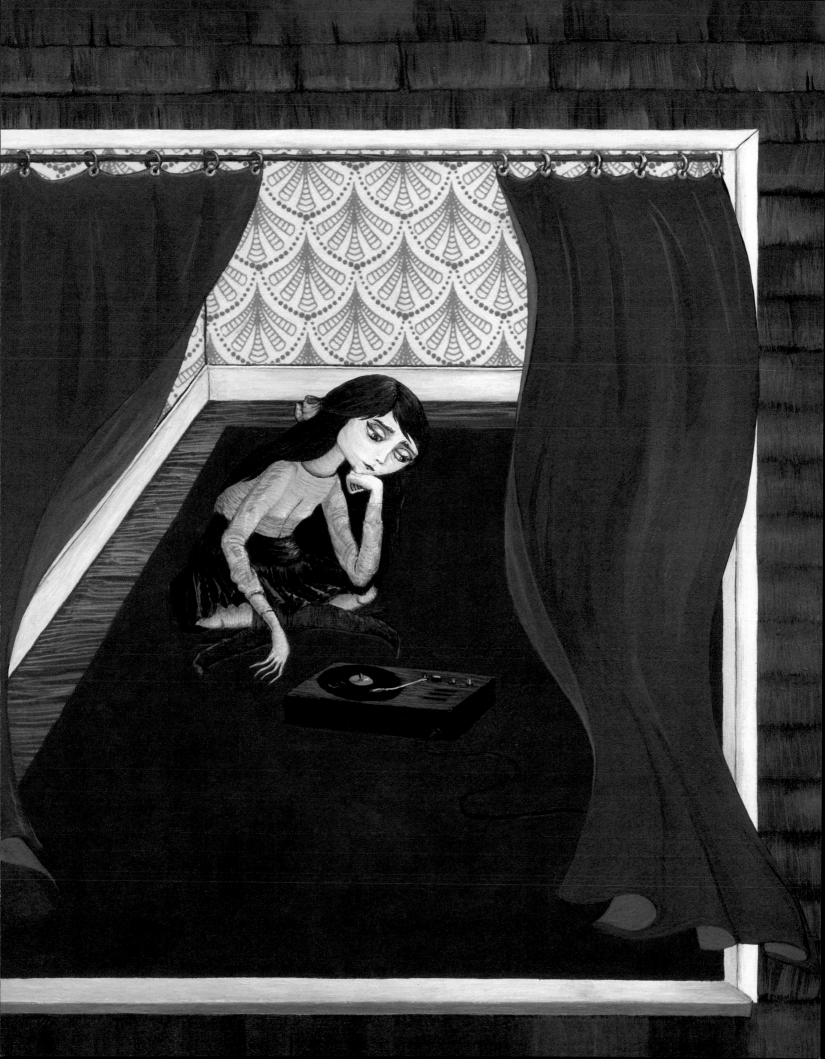

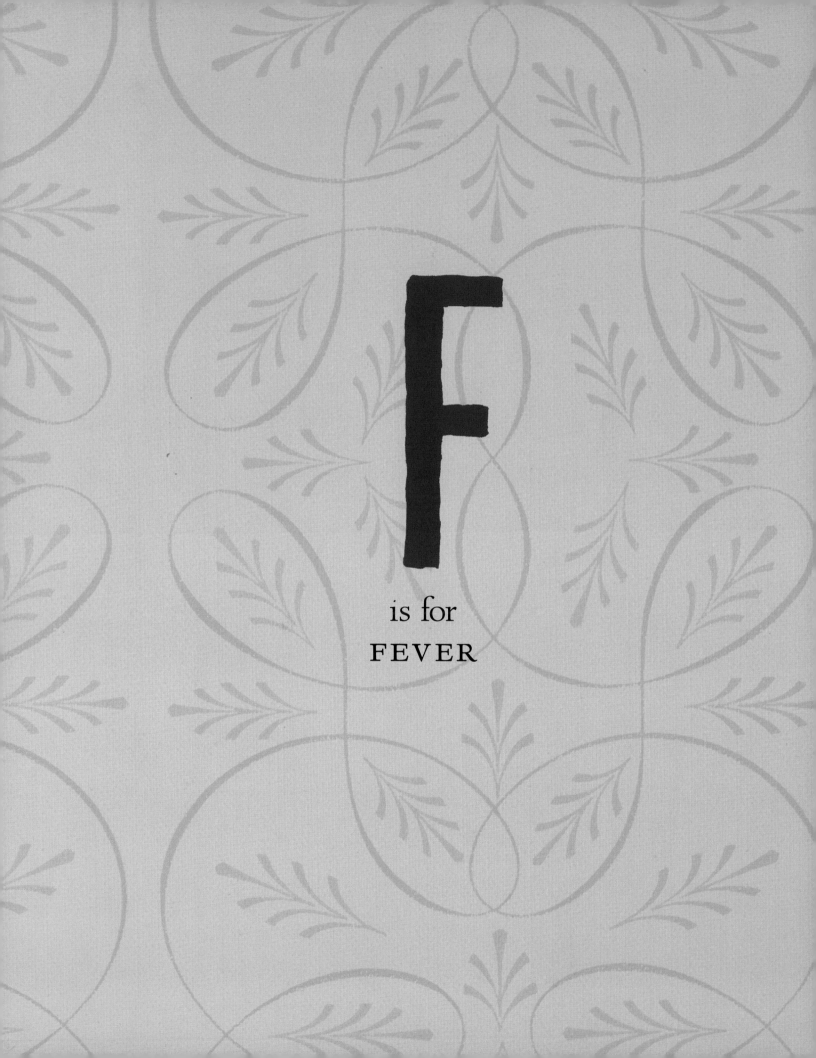

F

is for

FEVER

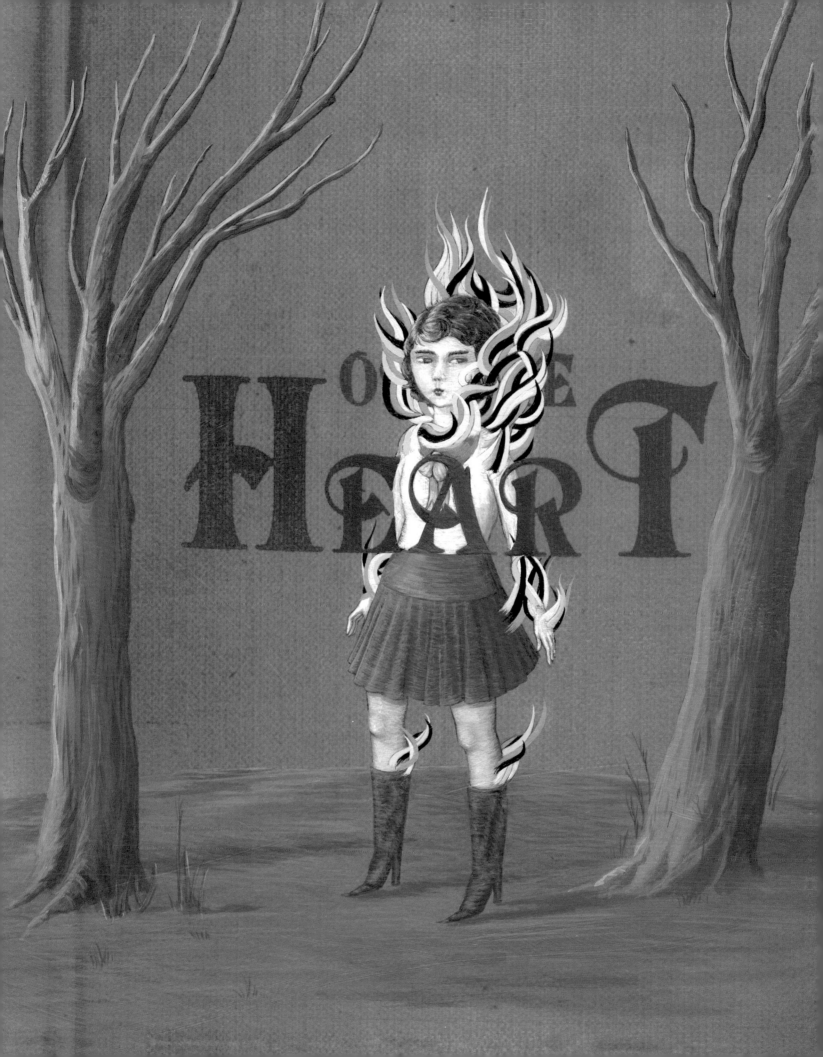

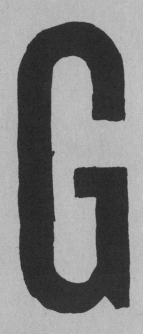

G

is for

GREMLINS

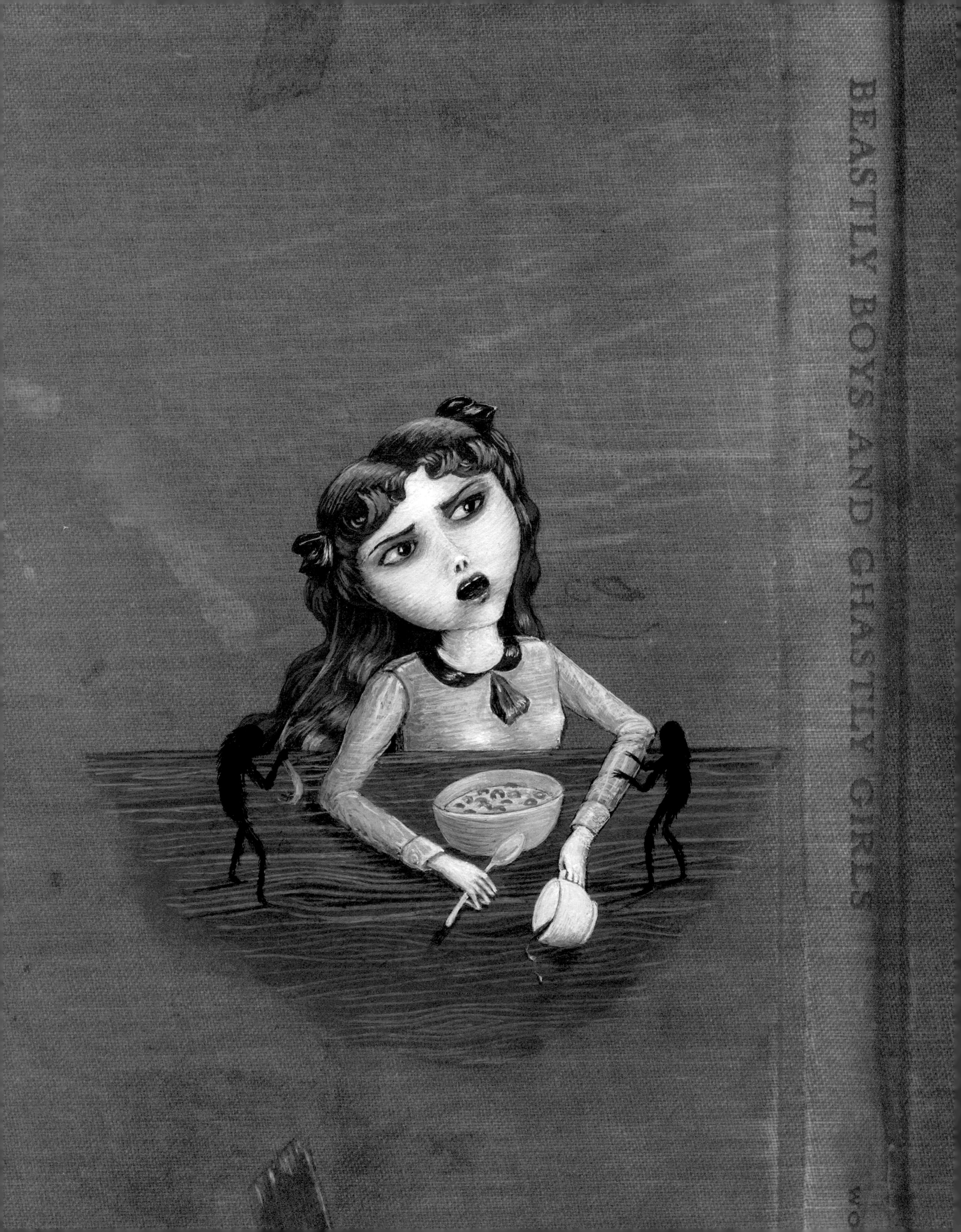
BEASTLY BOYS AND GHASTLY GIRLS

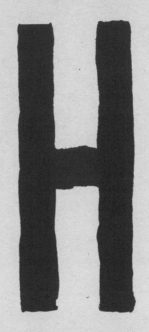

is for

HIDDEN

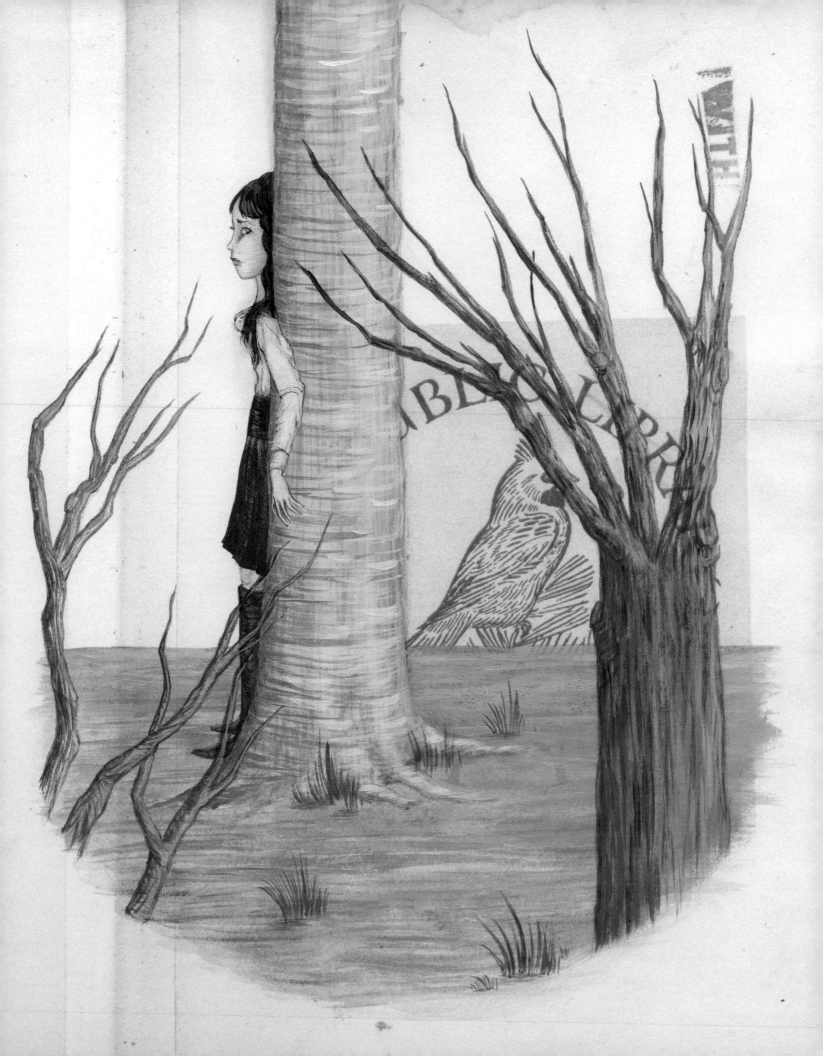

I

is for

INSOMNIA

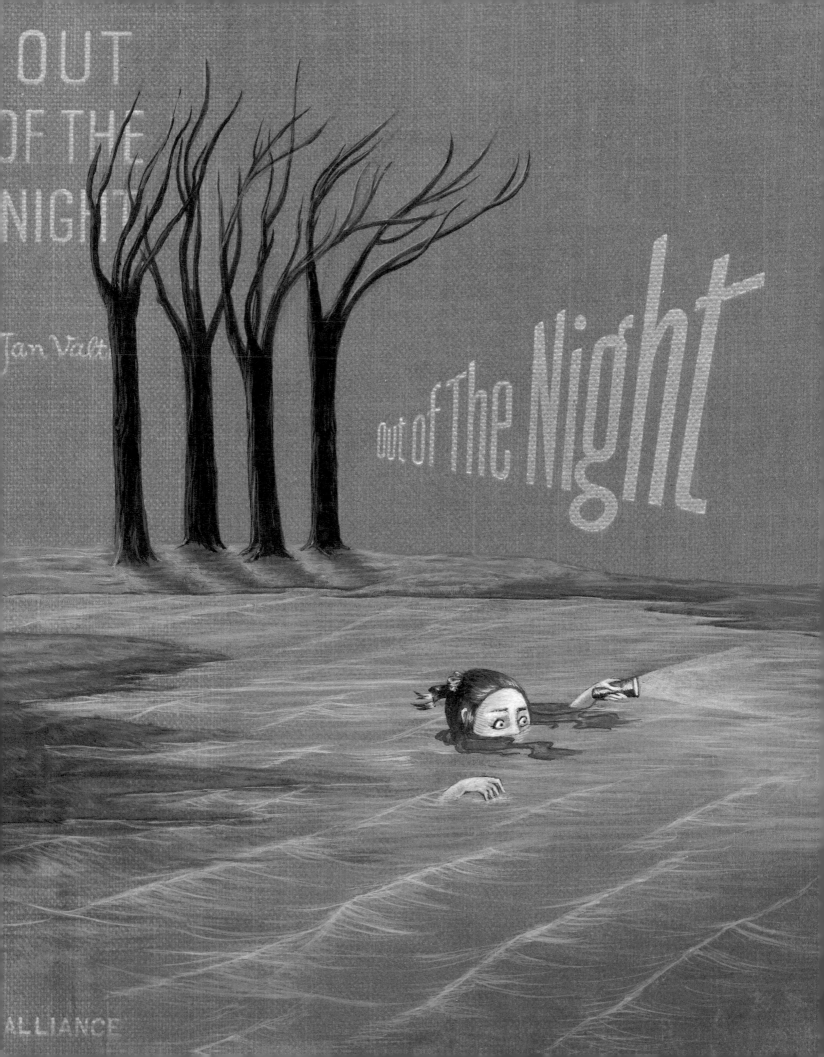

is for

JUVENILE DELINQUENT

The Gift of Little Things

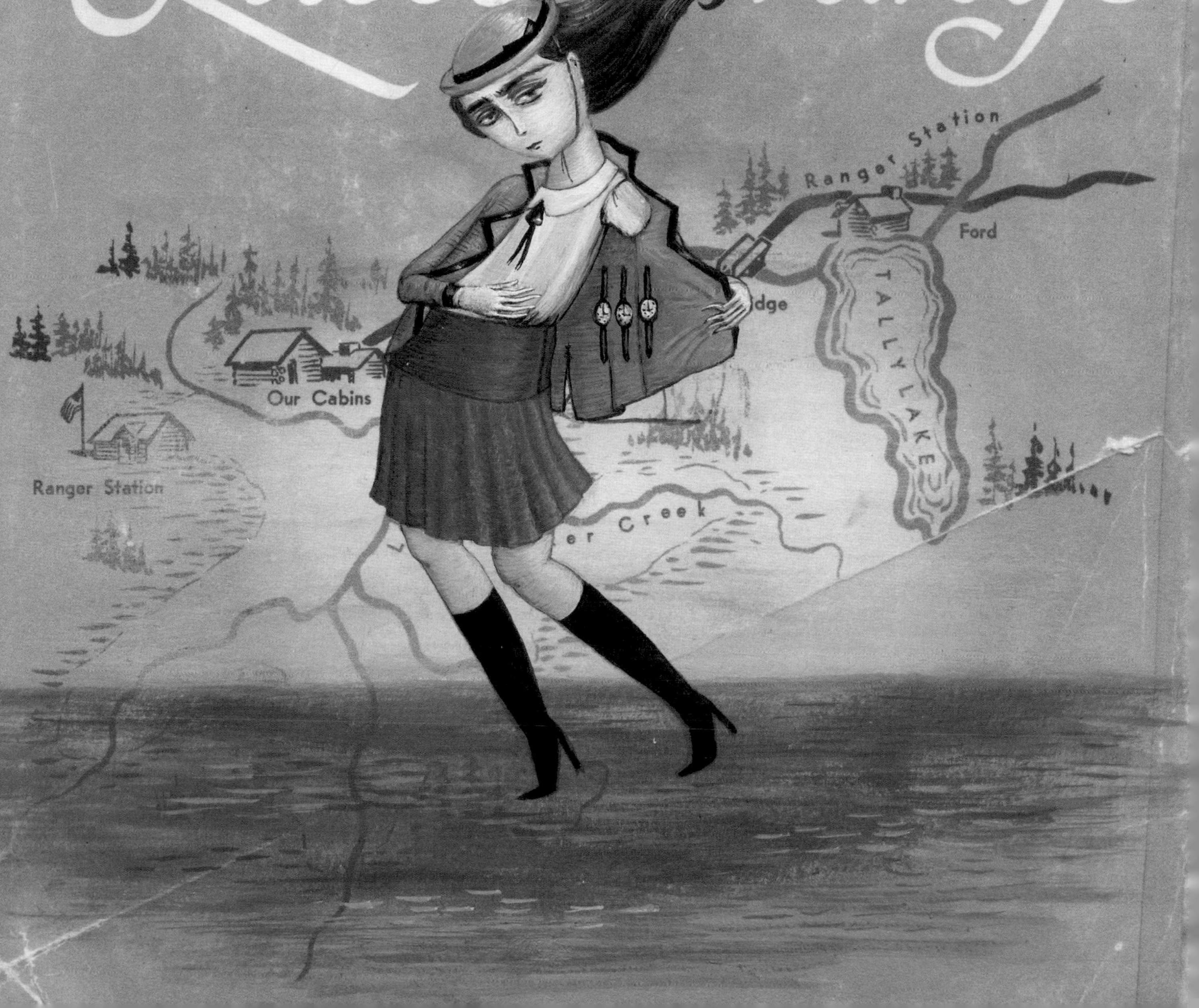

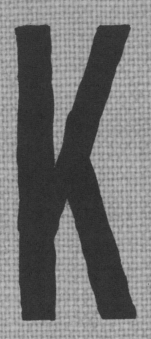

is for

KIDNAPPED

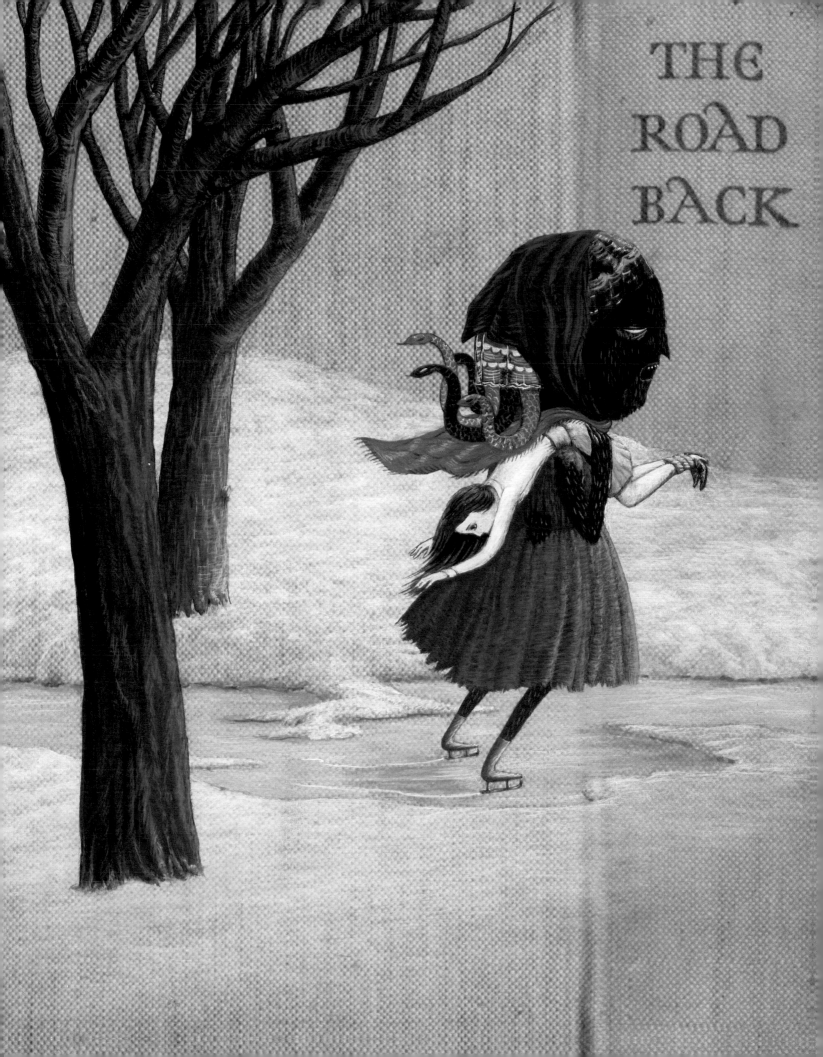

THE
ROAD
BACK

is for
LOST

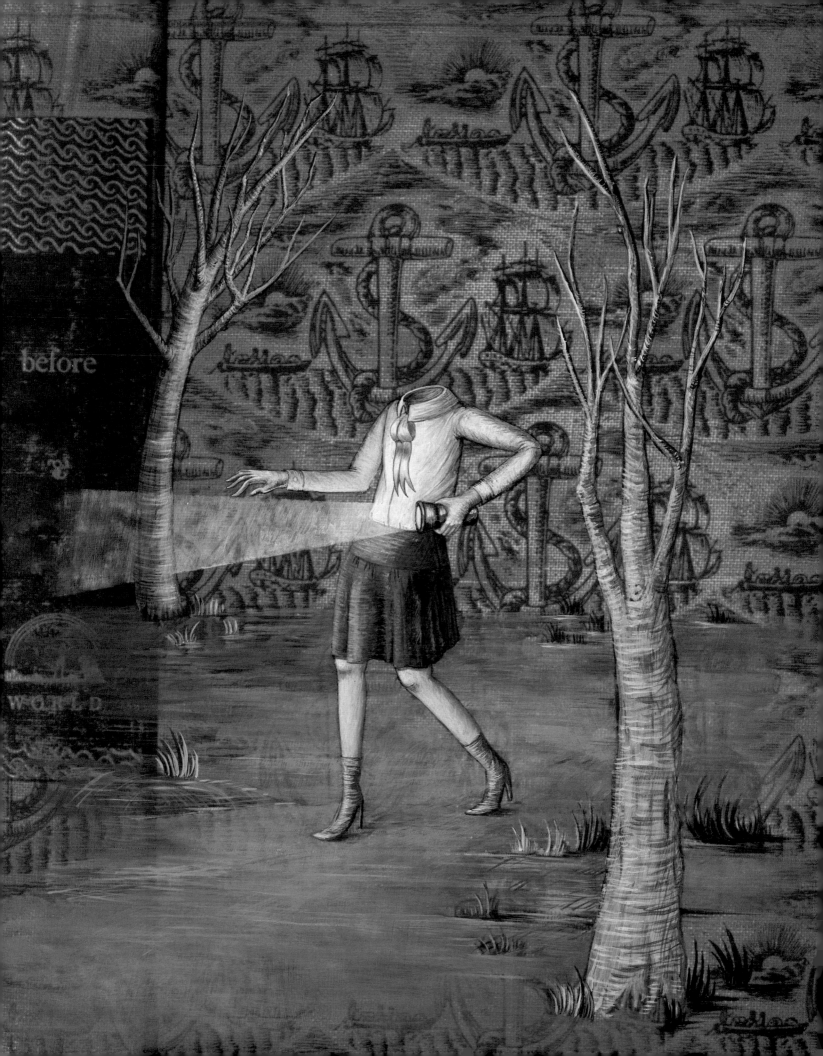

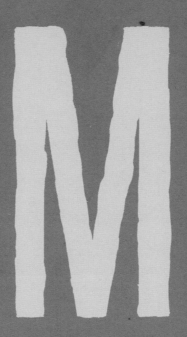

is for
MONONUCLEOSIS

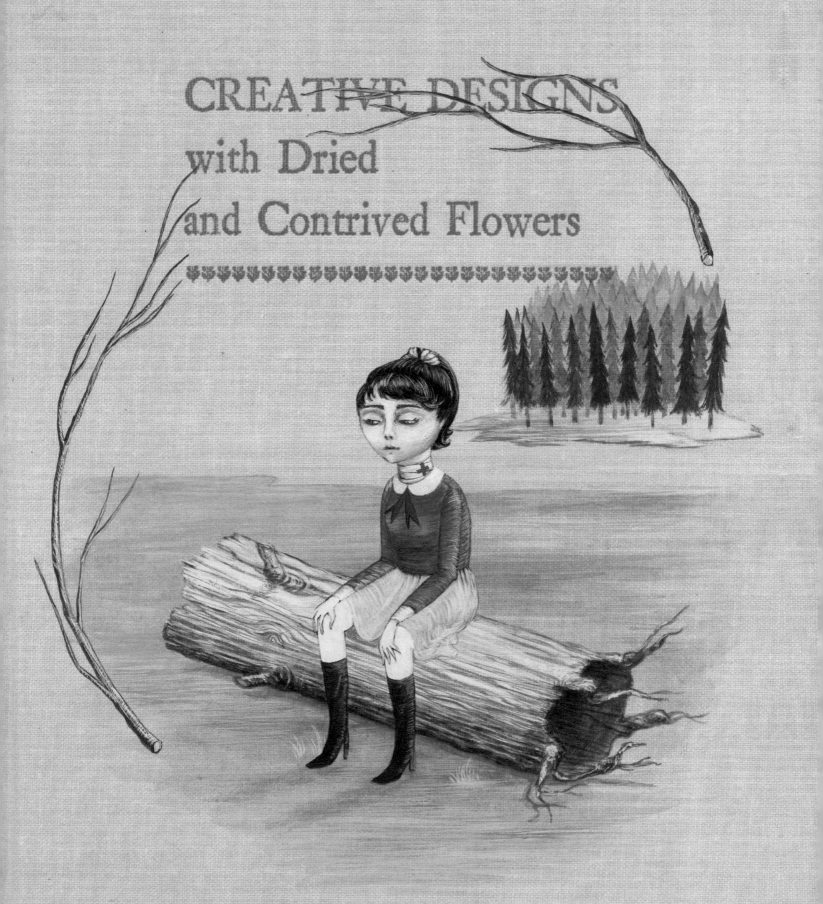

CREATIVE DESIGNS
with Dried
and Contrived Flowers

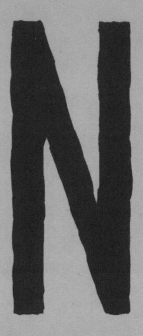

N

is for

NARCOLEPSY

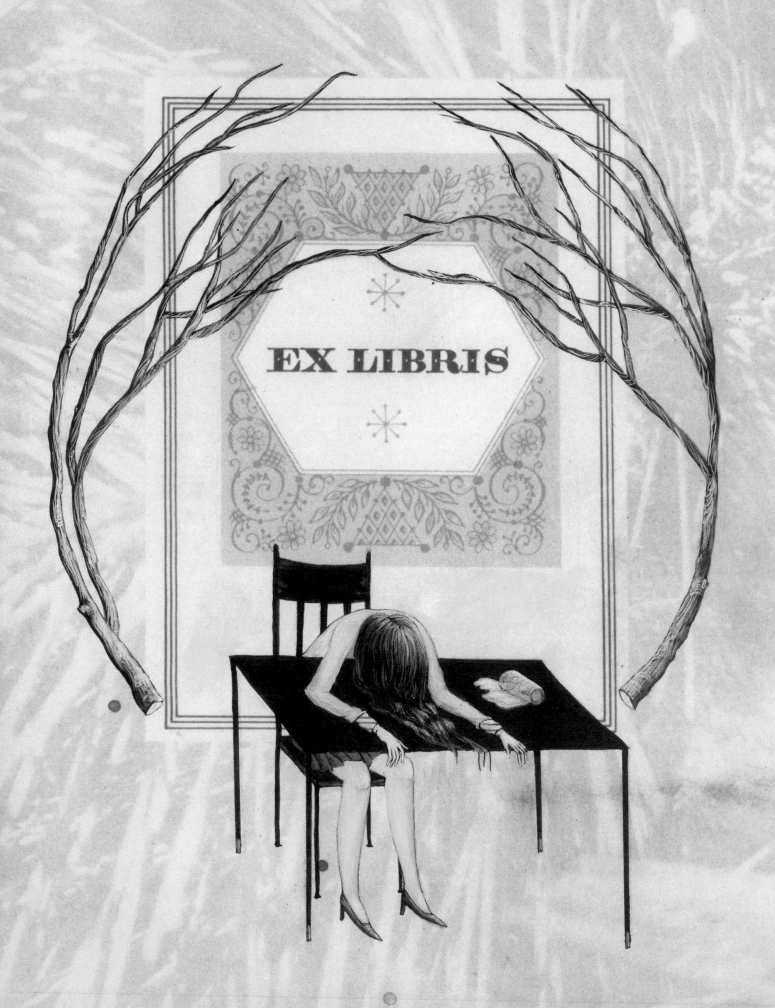

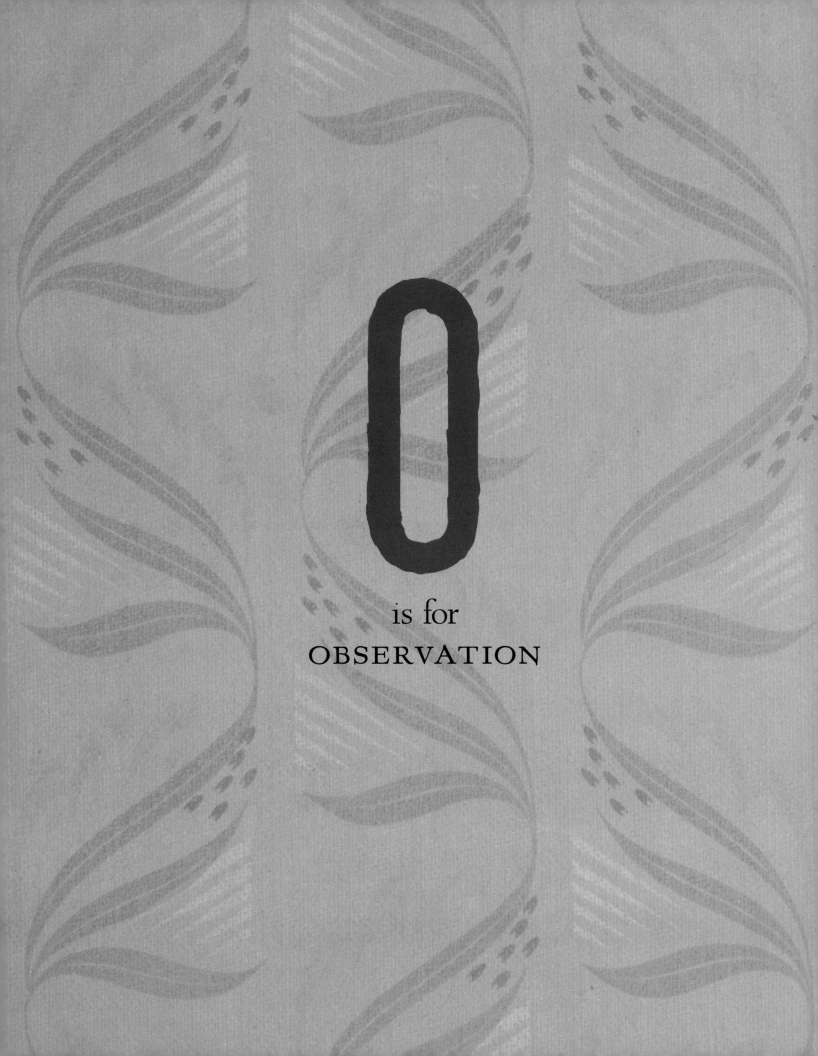

O

is for

OBSERVATION

A
PERFECT
SPY

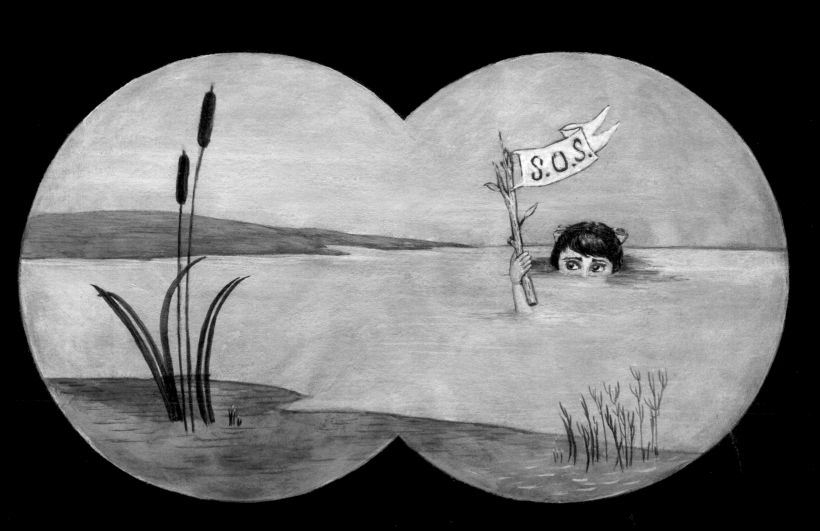

P

is for

PALE

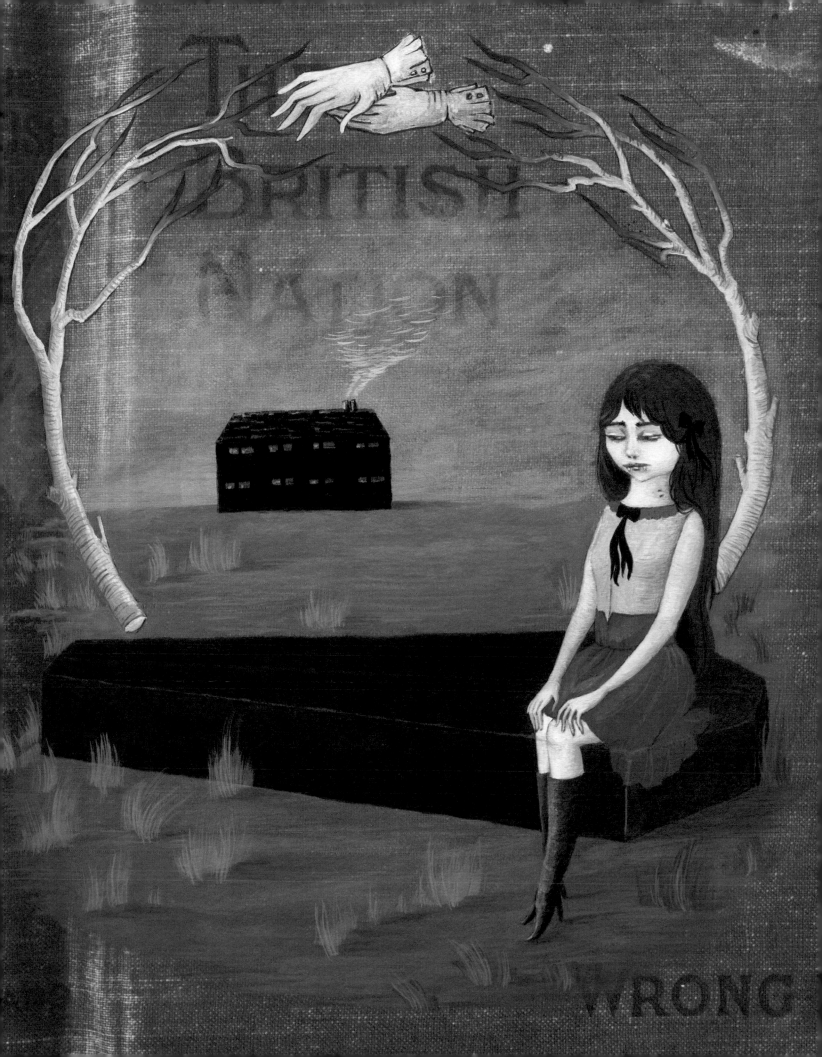

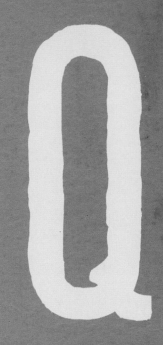

is for

QUARANTINE

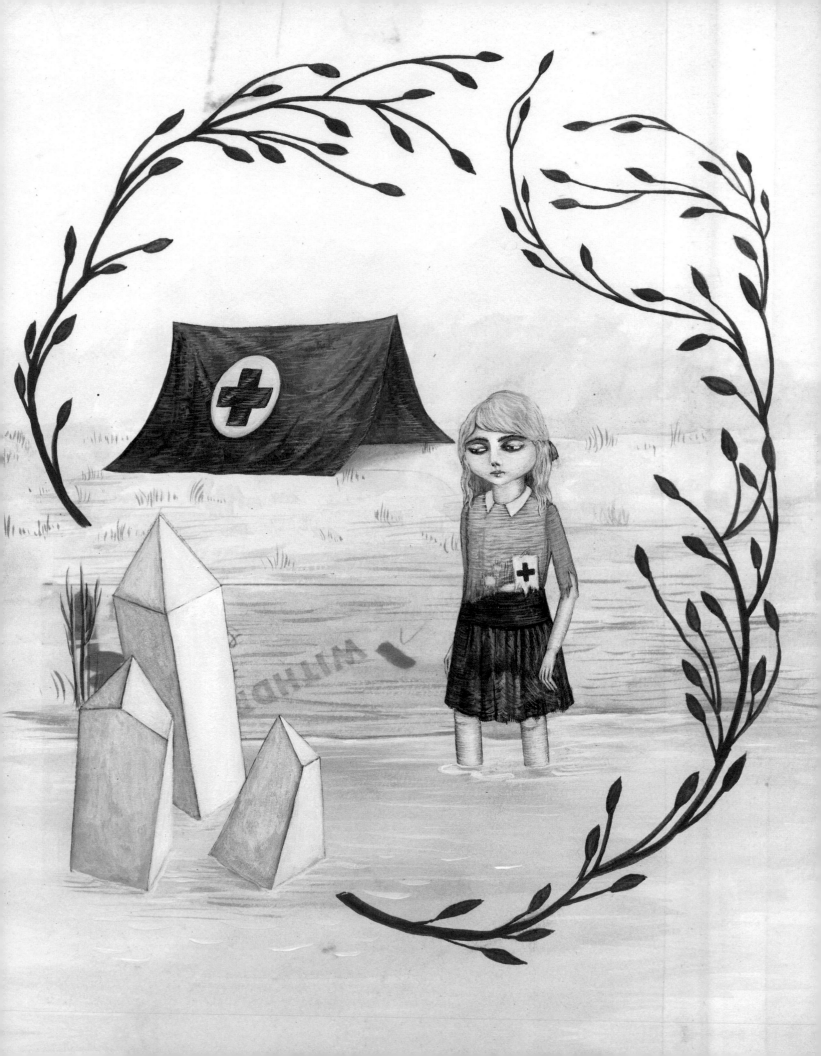

R

is for

REVENGE

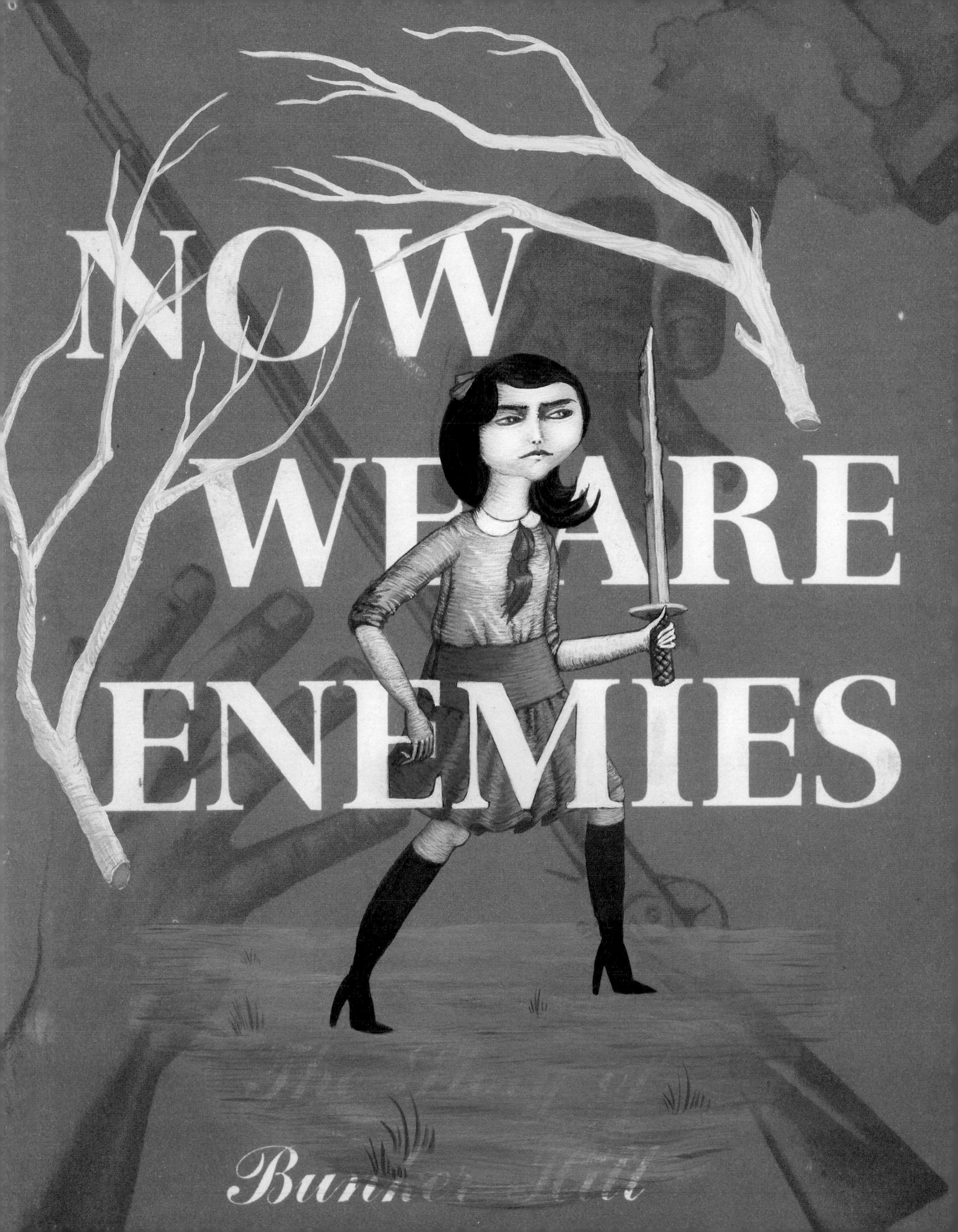
NOW
WE ARE
ENEMIES
Bunker Hill

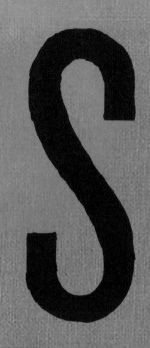

is for

SEPARATION ANXIETY

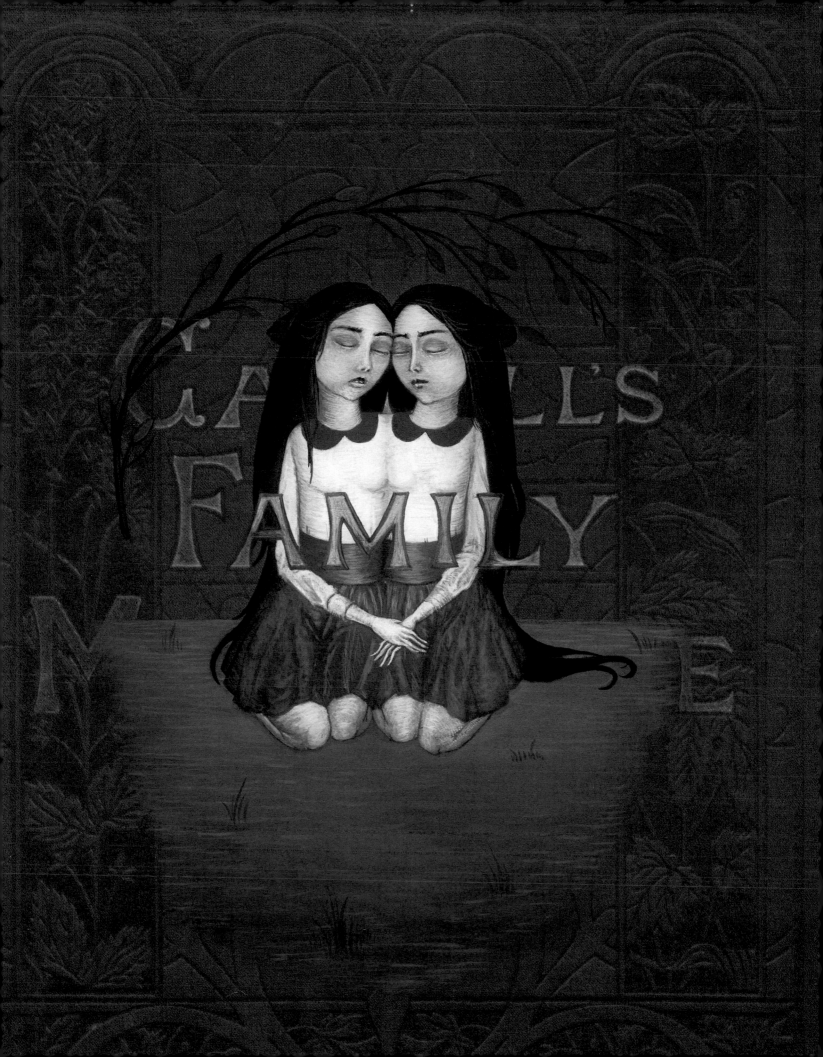

T

is for

TELEPORTATION

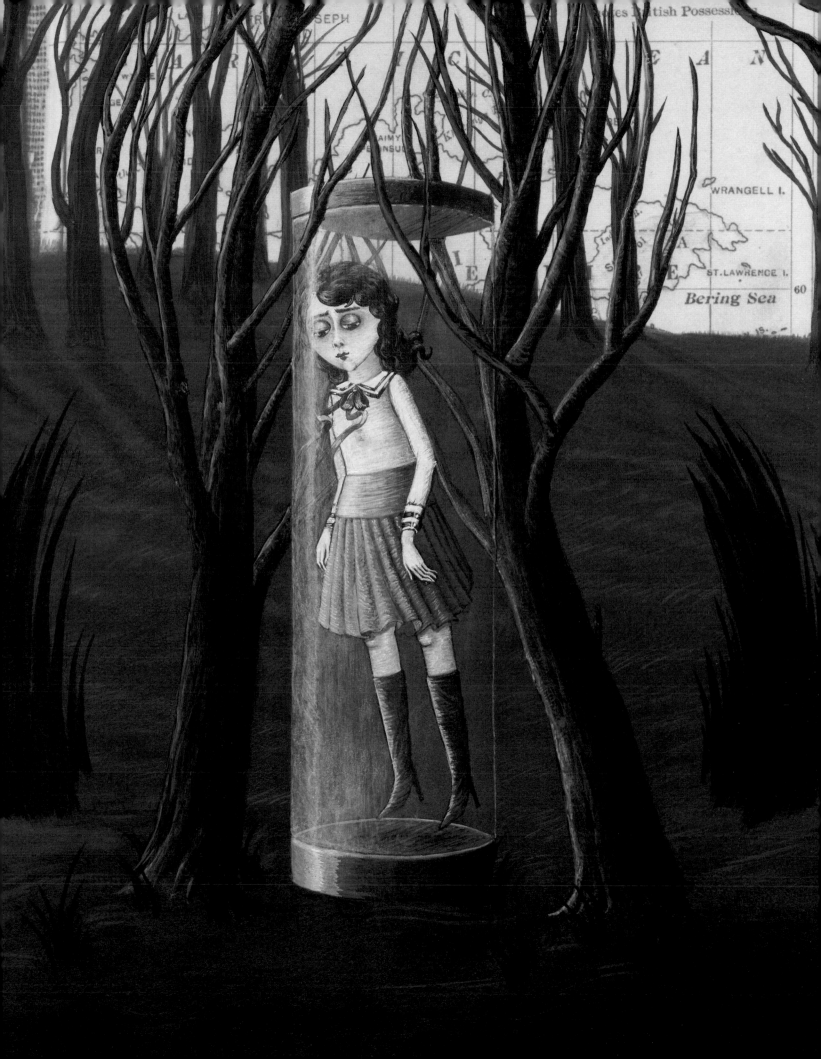

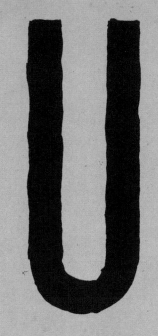

is for

UNSOLVED

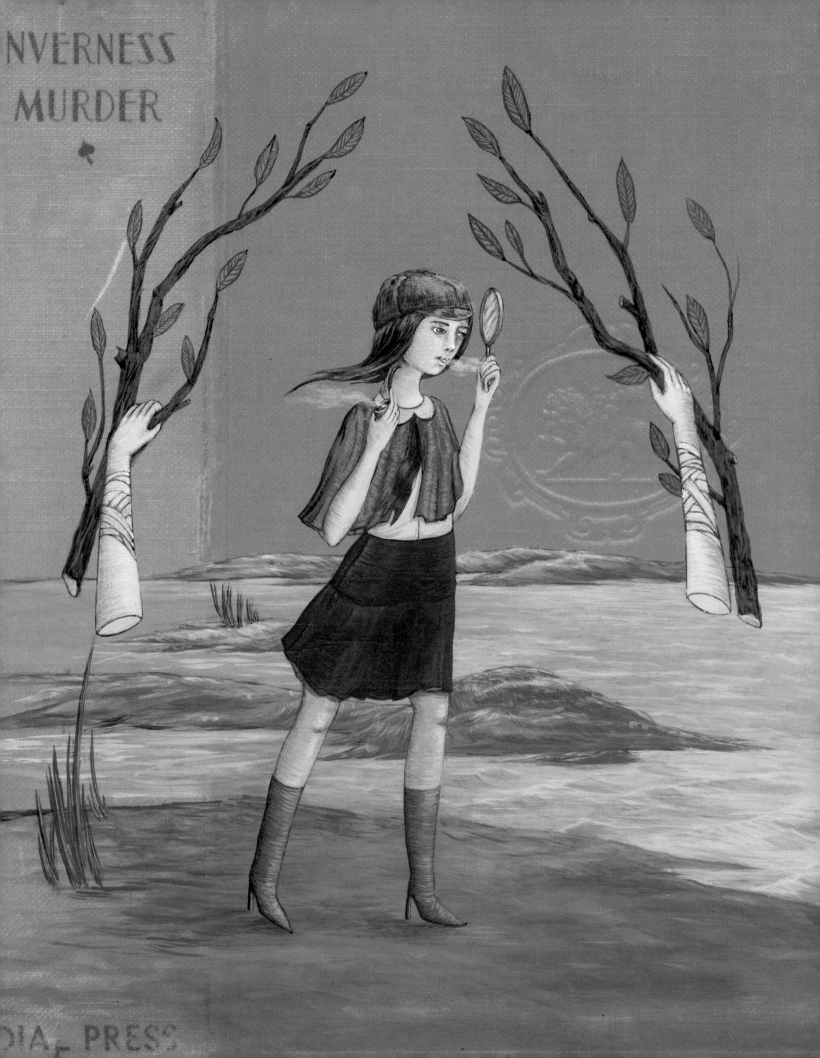

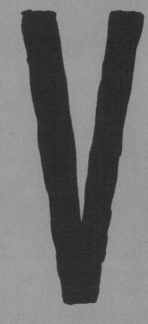

is for

VORTEX

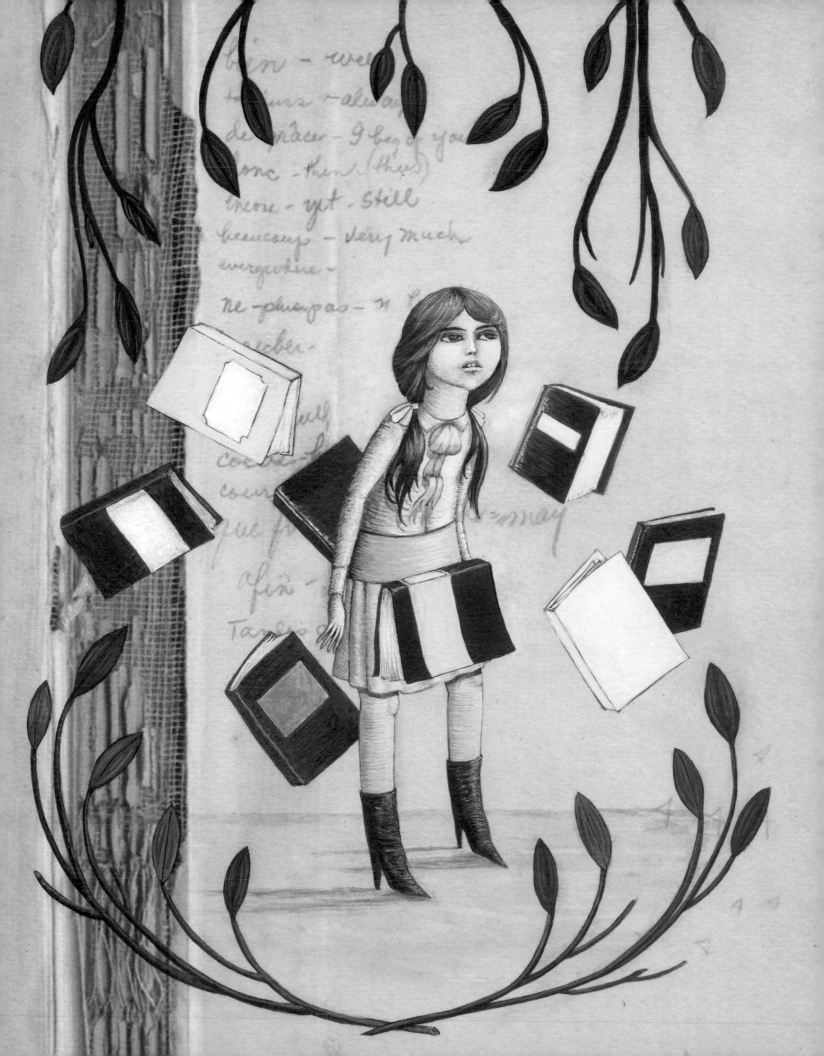

W

is for

WATERLOGGED

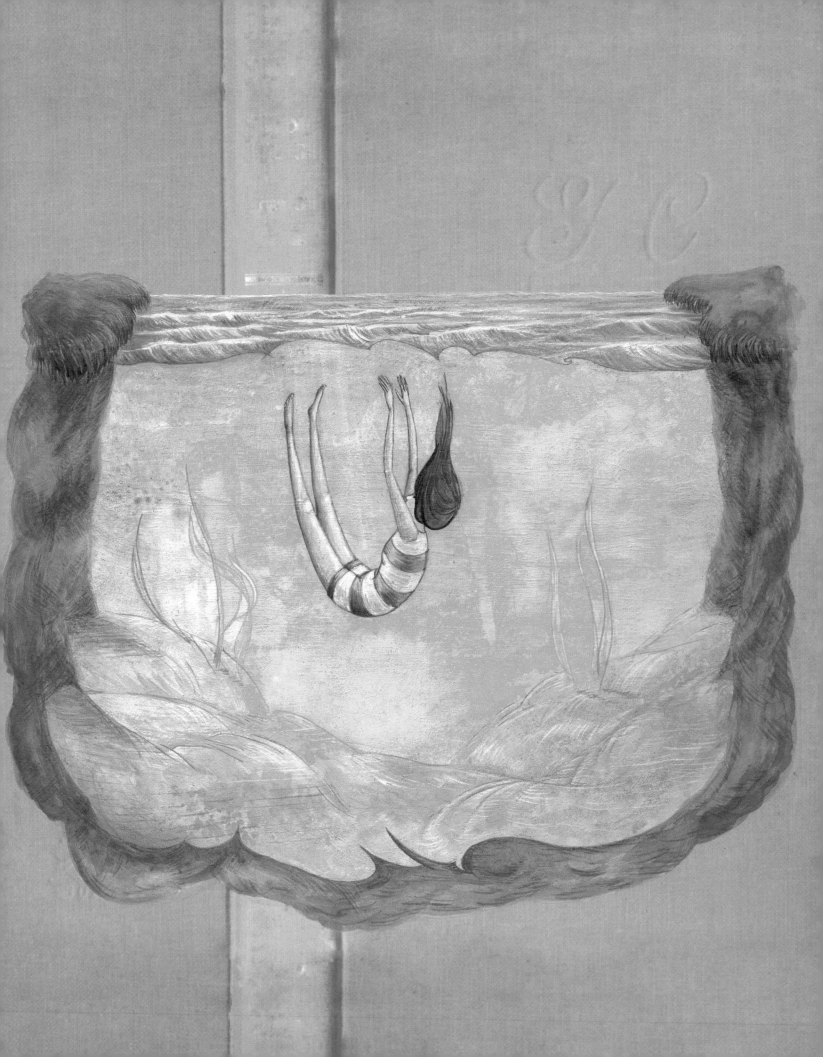

X

is for

X-RAY

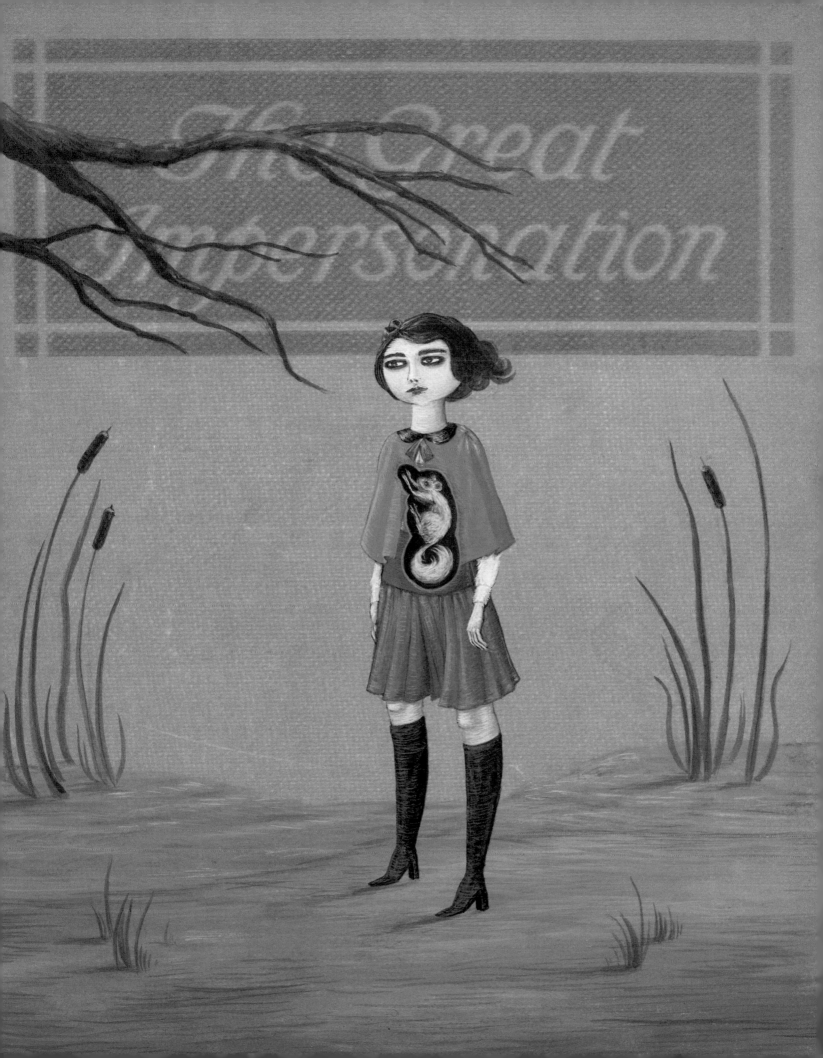

Y

is for
YETI

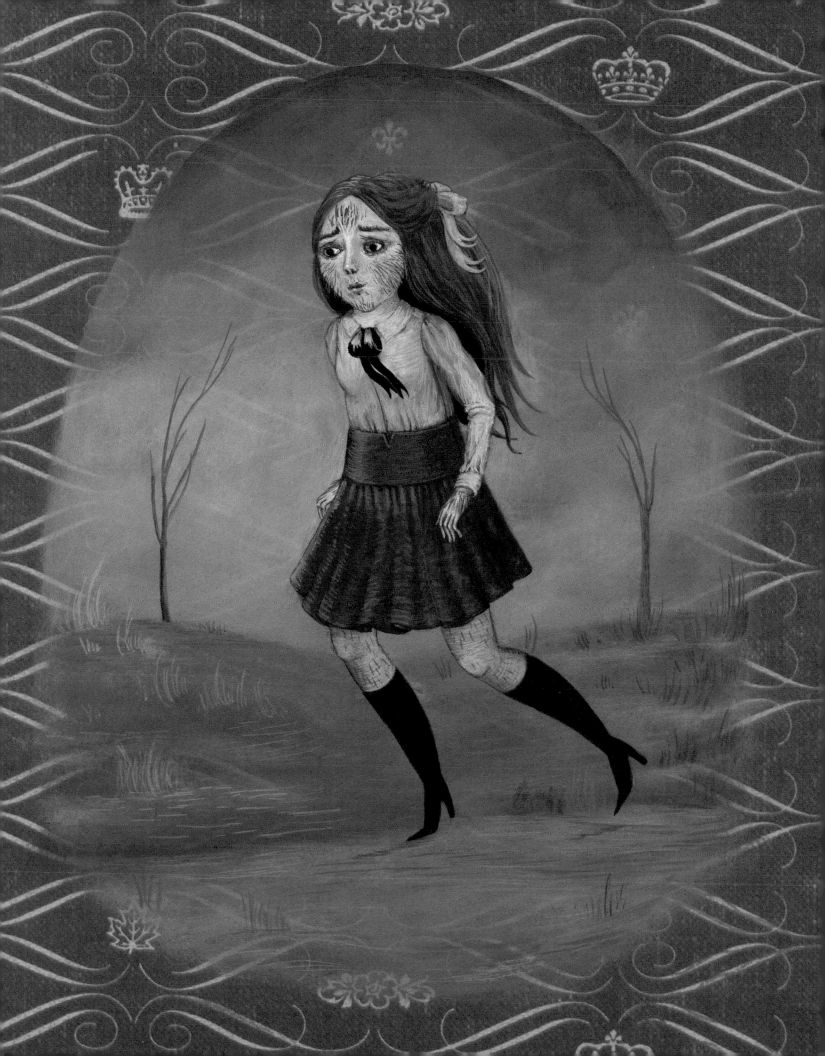

is for

ZOMBIE APOCALYPSE

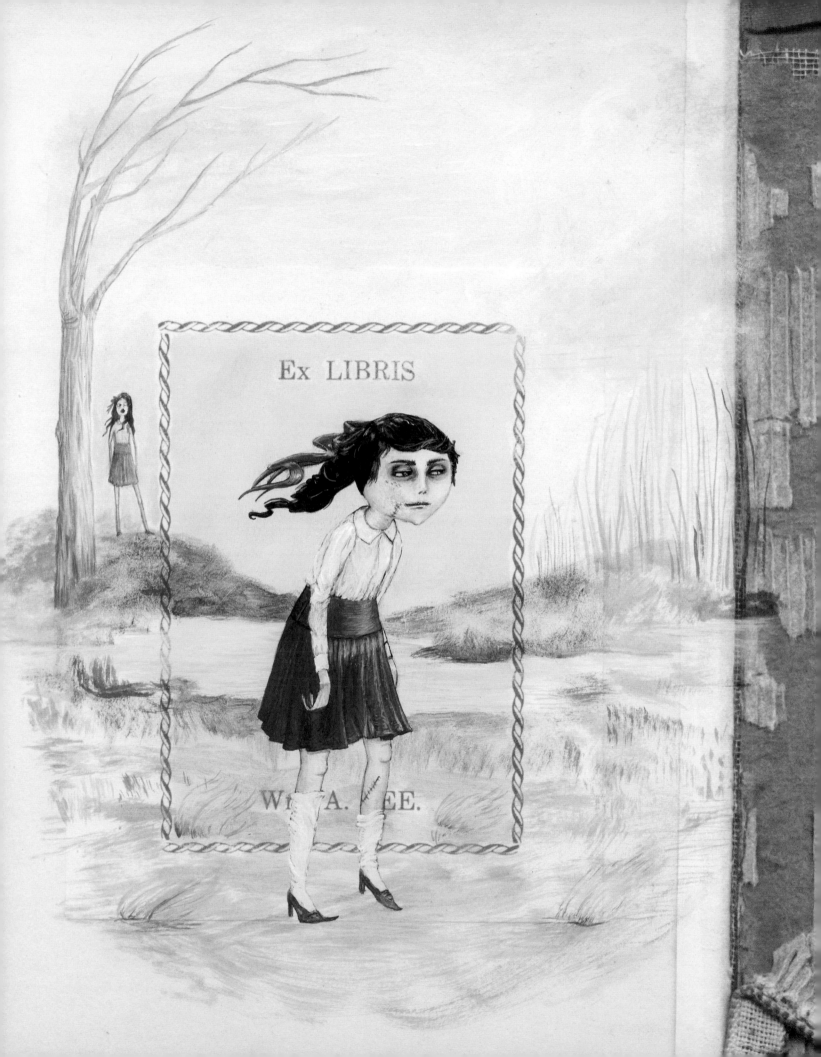

Ex LIBRIS

W A. EE.

Published in 2014 by Simply Read Books www.simplyreadbooks.com
Text & illustrations © 2014 Rebecca Chaperon

CIP Data available from Library and Archives Canada Cataloguing in Publication.

We gratefully acknowledge for their financial support of our publishing program the Canada Council
for the Arts, the BC Arts Council, and the Government of Canada through the Canada Book Fund (CBF).

Manufactured in Malaysia
Book design by Naomi MacDougall

10 9 8 7 6 5 4 3 2 1

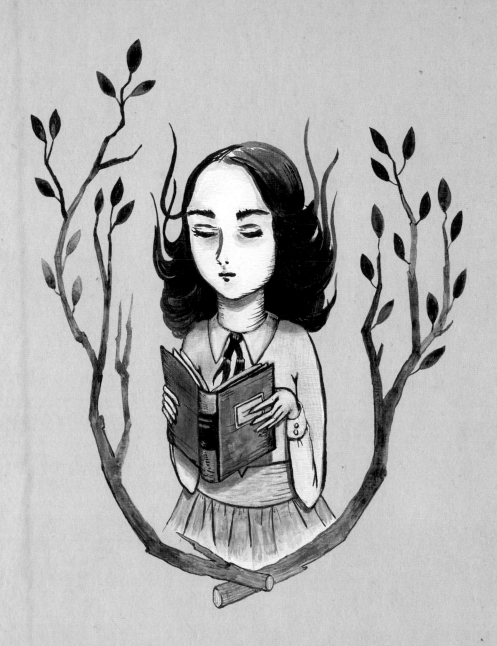

REBECCA CHAPERON'S fine art paintings capture the misadventures of various heroines from literary works while portraying the tale of a female protagonist within a surreal landscape. Her images entertain the mind with possible narratives, while haunting us with underlying emotions.

Rebecca lives in Vancouver, BC, Canada, with a handsome fella named Ben and an aloof orange cat named Dweezil. Please visit www.thechaperon.ca.

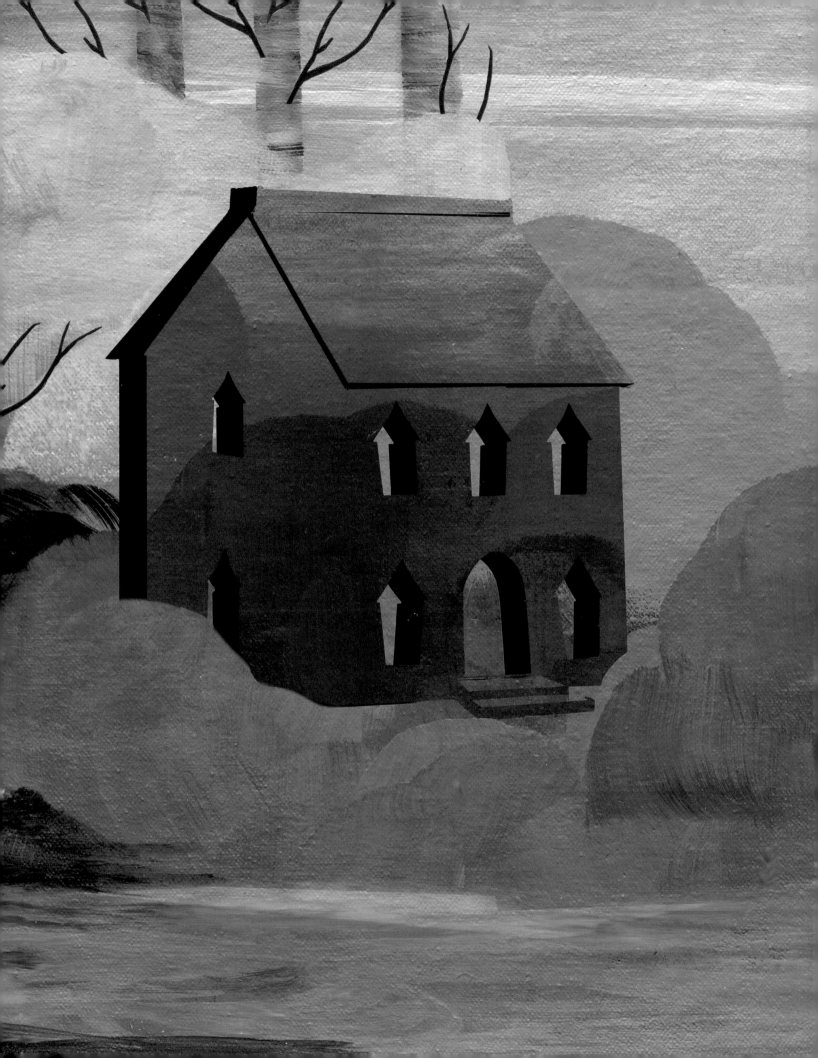